My First
Oxford
Book of
Stories

Geraldine McCaughrean

Illustrated by Ruby Green

OXFORD
UNIVERSITY PRESS

For Toby Bamber G.McC.

OXFORD
UNIVERSITY PRESS

Great Clarendon Street, Oxford OX2 6DP
Oxford University Press is a department of the University of Oxford.
It furthers the University's objective of excellence in research, scholarship,
and education by publishing worldwide in
Oxford New York

Athens Auckland Bangkok Bogotá Buenos Aires Calcutta
Cape Town Chennai Dar es Salaam Delhi Florence Hong Kong Istanbul
Karachi Kuala Lumpur Madrid Melbourne Mexico City Mumbai
Nairobi Paris São Paulo Shanghai Singapore Taipei Tokyo Toronto Warsaw
with associated companies in Berlin Ibadan
Oxford is a registered trade mark of Oxford University Press
in the UK and in certain other countries

British Library Cataloguing in Publication Data available

ISBN 0-19-278115 4 (hardback)
ISBN 0-19-278187 1 (paperback)

Printed in Spain by Gráficas Estella, S.A.

CONTENTS

LITTLE RED RIDING HOOD

❖

Once upon a time, there was a little girl who lived on the edge of a deep, dark wood. Whenever she went out, she wore a red velvet cloak with a red velvet hood. Her Grandmamma had made it for her, and that was why everyone called her Little Red Riding Hood.

One day, her mother told her: 'Your Grandmamma is ill. Take these pies and cakes and fruit to her cottage and tell her we all hope she's well again soon.'

Little Red Riding Hood had never been to her grandmother's cottage, for it was deep in the wood. But she took the basket of food, put on her red cloak and hood, and set off through the trees. 'Remember!' called her mother from the back step. 'Don't talk to any strangers and come straight home again!' But Red Riding Hood did not hear.

She had not gone far into the wood when she met a Big Bad Wolf. 'Good morning, Little Red Riding Hood,' said the Wolf politely. 'What have you got in the basket?'

'Pies and cakes and fruit for Grandmamma,' said Little Red Riding Hood. 'She's not very well.'

'I'm sorry to hear it. Does she live in the wood like me?'

'Yes, perhaps you know her. Her cottage is half an hour in that direction,' said Little Red Riding Hood, and she pointed through the trees.

'Ah, yes.' The Wolf grinned. 'A dear old lady.'

He looked into the basket. 'Hm. If I were sick, I know a bunch of flowers would cheer me up. Why don't you pick some of those?' And he pointed out a pool of primroses splashing the forest floor with yellow.

'Oh yes!' cried Red Riding Hood and, setting down her basket, she began to pick primroses. It took a long time to make a nice bouquet. And then, as Little Red Riding Hood went on down the path, she stopped to watch the squirrels and birds playing in the trees.

So the Big Bad Wolf, loping through the trees, reached Grandmamma's cottage before her, and knocked on the door.

'Who's there?' called a frail little voice.

'It's me, Grandmamma!' piped the Wolf. 'It's me— Little Red Riding Hood.'

'Lift the latch, open the door, and walk in, my dear,' said Grandmamma. 'I'm too poorly to get out of bed.'

So in went the Wolf—over the threshold, over the rug, over the foot of the bed. And he wolfed down Grandmamma, shawl and all. Only her lace nightcap fell to the floor. The Wolf pulled on the nightcap over his pointed ears, put out the light and, climbing into bed, pulled the sheets right up to his hairy chin.

Knock, knock, knock. Little Red Riding Hood knocked at the door of Grandmamma's cottage.

'Who's there?' called a frail little voice.

'It's me, Grandmamma. It's me— Little Red Riding Hood.'

'Lift the latch, open the door, and walk in, my dear,' said the voice. 'I'm too poorly to get out of bed.'

So in went Little Red Riding Hood.

And there in the bed sat a shadowy figure, the sheets drawn up high, the pillows plumped up behind. 'Come closer, my dear,' said the shadowy figure. 'Let me see what you've brought.'

'It's very dark in here,' said Little Red Riding Hood, stroking Grandmamma's hand. It was a very hairy hand, and its nails were very long. Leaning closer, she was surprised to see two yellow eyes beneath Grandmamma's white lace nightcap.

'Oh, Grandmamma, what big eyes you've got!'

'All the better to see you with, my dear,' Grandmamma laughed, and her nightcap slipped.

'Oh, Grandmamma, what big ears you've got!'

'All the better to hear you with, my dear.'

'Oh, Grandmamma,
what big hands you've got!'
'All the better to hug
you with, my dear.'

'But, Grandmamma,
what big teeth you've got!'

'All the better to EAT you
with, my dear!' cried the Wolf,
and, throwing back the
bedclothes, he chased Little
Red Riding Hood and caught
her and wolfed her down,
cloak and basket and all.
Only her red hood fell to
the floor.

After eating Grandmamma and Red Riding Hood, the Wolf felt very full and sleepy. He lay down on the bed and was soon fast asleep, his snores shaking the glass in the windows and the pictures in their frames.

A woodcutter happened to be passing the cottage, and heard this strange noise. 'Oh, dear, I hope old Granny Hood isn't ill,' he thought, and looked in through the window. When he saw the Wolf and the lace cap and the red hood, he guessed at once what had happened. So he lifted the latch, opened the door, and walked in.

Over to the bed he went, and cut open the Wolf with the sharp blade of his knife. Out jumped Red Riding Hood and Grandmamma, too. But the woodcutter put his finger to his lips. 'Shshsh!'

On tiptoe they crept outside to the garden and fetched a stone in each hand—six stones, which they carried indoors and put into the Wolf's stomach. Then

Grandmamma sewed shut the slit, and they all three hid in the wardrobe.

'My! But eating people makes you thirsty!' declared the Wolf as he woke up and stretched himself. 'I'm off to the river for a drink.'

So he jumped down from the bed. But with the six stones inside him, his front feet went one way and his back feet went another, and he fell splat-flat and tumbled out of the door, out of the forest, out of the land.

And *that* was the end of the Big Bad Wolf.

The woodcutter packed up his gun and strode back into the wood. Grandmamma set a tea of pies and cakes and fruit, with a vase in the middle for the primroses. They were so pretty that they made her feel quite better. And even though Little Red Riding Hood stayed for tea, she set off well before dark and got home safe and sound.

And afterwards, whenever she walked in the deep, dark wood, she never spoke to strangers again.

THE BILLY GOATS GRUFF

❖

There were once three billy goats—big old Grandfather Gruff, his son Bill, and his grandson Billy who was hardly more than a kid. They spent the snowy winter in a valley. But when spring came, they longed to climb to the green alps where sweet grass grew.

As they set off, the little bell on the littlest Billy Goat Gruff went *ting tang tong*, and his little feet went *trit trat trot*.

The bell on the second Billy Goat Gruff went *cling clong clang,* and his feet went *clippity-clip.*

But the big bell on the biggest Billy Goat Gruff went *bing bang bong* and his big feet went *clip-clop clip-clop.*

'Soon we will cross the river gorge and reach the mountains,' he said.

Little did they know that a terrible troll had made his home under the bridge. There was no other way across the gorge, and the troll was growing fat and happy, eating the travellers who passed that way.

As the littlest Billy Goat Gruff came trotting over the bridge, his bell went *ting tang tong* and his feet went *trit trat trot.* The troll heard him and poked his red eyes over the edge of the bridge.

'Who dares to cross my bridge?' he said. 'I'll eat him between bread for a sandwich!'

The littlest Billy Goat Gruff blinked at the troll, then he said, 'Eat me if you must, but I'm very small and thin. My father, Billy Goat Gruff, is coming along behind me. He's much bigger and fatter than I am. Listen.'

'Hrmph,' said the troll, but he listened, and sure enough he could hear the second Billy Goat Gruff coming, his bell going *cling clong clang.* 'All right, be off with you,' said the troll. 'But I'll be waiting to eat you up on your way back.'

So the littlest Billy Goat Gruff hurried on across the bridge. But he stopped at the far side, to see what would happen.

The second Billy Goat Gruff reached the bridge, and his feet went *clippity-clip* and the bell round his neck went *cling clong clang*. The troll poked his bulging blue nose over the edge of the bridge. 'Who dares to cross my bridge? I'll eat him under pastry for a pie!'

The second Billy Goat Gruff blinked at the troll, then he said, 'Eat me if you must, but I'm rather bony and tough. My father, Billy Goat Gruff, is coming along behind me. He's much bigger and fatter than I. Listen.'

'Hrrmmphph!' said the troll, but he listened, and sure enough he could hear the third Billy Goat Gruff coming, his bell going *bing bang bong*. 'All right,' said the troll. 'Get off my bridge. But I'll be waiting here to eat you up on your way back!'

So the second Billy Goat Gruff hurried on across the bridge. But he stopped at the far side as well, to see what would happen.

When the third Billy Goat Gruff reached the bridge, his feet went *clip-clop clip-clop* and the bell round his neck went *bing bang bong*. The troll pulled himself on to the bridge and stood barring the way—and a nasty, nobbly, spiteful, spikey, horrible, hairy troll he was. 'Who DARES to cross MY bridge? I'll eat him RAW!'

The biggest Billy Goat Gruff blinked at the troll, then he said, 'Eat me, will you? We'll see about that!' And he lowered his two great horns, and pawed the planks with his big front foot—*ratch scratch scrape*—

'I've horns on my head and hooves on my feet
And I'll show you what they're for!
I've got hooves on my feet and horns on my head:
I've seen worse than *you* before!'

Then he thundered over the bridge and rammed the troll, and tossed him so high in the air that the troll did not come down for three days.

So the third Billy Goat Gruff reached the other side of the bridge, and trotted into the mountains with his son and grandson, to eat the sweet grass all summer long.

For all I know, they may still be there.

THE THREE LITTLE PIGS

❖

A mother and her three baby pigs lived together in a comfortable sty. But as the pigs grew bigger, the space between them grew smaller until there was no room for them all.

'Off you go, and build houses of your own,' said their mother. 'But beware of the Big Bad Wolf.'

So the first little pig built a house out of straw, with a straw roof and straw walls and a straw door. It took no time at all, and when it was finished it was as snug as any haystack.

The second little pig built a house out of sticks, with wicker walls, a roof of twigs, and a bamboo door. It took a bit longer, but when it was finished it was as snug as any robin's nest.

The third little pig built his house out of brick, with a brick chimney, slates on the roof, and a big oak door. It took a long time, but when it was finished it was as snug as, well, your house or mine.

Not one day later, the Big Bad Wolf called at the straw house.

'Little pig, little pig, let me come in!'

'No, not by the hairs on my chinny-chin-chin—

I won't let you in,' replied the little pig.

'You won't? Then I'll huff and I'll puff and I'll blow your house down!'

So the Big Bad Wolf huffed and puffed and he blew . . . The straw house blew all to pieces, and the little pig ran *whee-whee-whee-whee!* all the way to the stick house. Right on his heels came the Wolf!

No sooner had the two little pigs locked and barred the door, than the Wolf hammered on it.

'Little pigs, little pigs, let me come in!'

'No, not by the hairs on my chinny-chin-chin—

I won't let you come in,' replied the second little pig.

'You won't? Then I'll huff and I'll puff and I'll *blow* your house down!'

So the Big Bad Wolf huffed and he puffed and he puffed and he *blew* . . . The stick house collapsed like a pack of cards, and the two little pigs ran *whee-whee-whee-whee!* all the way to the brick house. Right on their heels came the Wolf!

No sooner had the three little pigs locked and barred the big oak door, than the Wolf hammered on it.

'Little pigs, little pigs, let me come in!'

'No, not by the hairs on my chinny-chin-chin— I WON'T let you in,' replied the third little pig.

'You won't? Then I'll huff and I'll puff and I'll BLOW your house down!'

So the Big Bad Wolf huffed and he puffed and he huffed and he puffed and he huffed and he puffed and he blew, *blew*, BLEW! But though he blew till his whiskers wilted and his tail drooped, the Big Bad Wolf could not get in. 'Drat!' thought the Wolf.

So he stopped huffing and puffing and he knocked gently on the door. 'I only wanted to tell you about the turnips in Farmer George's field,' he said through the keyhole. 'Why don't we meet bright and early and steal them together?'

'I like turnips,' replied the third little pig.

Now the Big Bad Wolf was planning to pounce on the little pig and eat him up, and the little pig guessed as much. He got up even brighter and even earlier, and went to the turnip field and fetched home all the best turnips before the Wolf was even out of bed.

'Drat!' said the Wolf, when he found the turnips gone. But he went back to the brick house and shouted through the keyhole, 'The apples are ripe in Farmer George's orchard. Meet you there bright and early, and we'll pick them together.'

'I'm particularly fond of apples,' replied the third little pig.

Now the Big Bad Wolf was planning to pounce on the little pig and eat him up, and the little pig guessed as much. He got up even brighter and even earlier, and went to the orchard to pick apples.

But this time the Big Bad Wolf was determined not to be

tricked. He, too, got to the orchard early.

The little pig was up in an apple tree and dared not climb down. Instead, he picked a juicy red apple and munched on it. 'Mmm, these apples are delicious, Mr Wolf. I'll throw them down to you.'

He threw one apple and the Wolf caught it.

He threw one just out of reach, and the Wolf ran, paw outstretched, and caught it.

Then the little pig threw an apple as far as he could throw it, and while the Wolf ran to fetch it, the little pig slid down the tree and ran home as fast as his little legs would carry him. Hot on his heels came the Wolf!

Into the brick house rushed the little pig, and slammed the big oak door. 'Drat!' said the Wolf, and called through the keyhole. 'You left before I could tell you about the fair!'

'The fair?' said the third little pig.

'Yes, there's a fair tomorrow in town. We could go

together. Meet you at the crossroads, bright and early.'

'Fairs are fun,' said the little pig.

Now the Big Bad Wolf was planning to pounce on the little pig and eat him up, and the little pig guessed as much. He got up much much brighter and far far earlier, and set off for town.

He had a wonderful time at the fair. He even won a shiny new butter churn. 'I can use it to cook in,' he thought.

But on the way back, he came over the hill and saw the Wolf still waiting at the crossroads. So, climbing into the churn, the little pig rolled and rocked it until the churn began to roll down the hill . . . faster and faster and faster . . .

The Wolf looked up to see something big and shiny hurtling towards him. He ran . . . but he could not run as fast as the butter churn was rolling . . .

Splat! It bowled him over and did not stop rolling until it reached the door of the brick house, and the pig jumped out.

'Drat and double drat!' said the Wolf, as he picked

himself up. 'That pig has got to go!'

He ran to the brick house. With a leap and a bound he scrambled on to the slate roof and crept towards the chimney. 'I'm coming to get you, little pigs! Nothing will save you now!'

'Oh dear, oh dear!' squealed the first little pig.

'Oh my, oh my!' squeaked the second little pig. But the third little pig was busy putting water into the butter churn. He set the pot over the fire to boil.

'I'm coming to eat you up!' called the Big Bad Wolf, climbing into the chimney pot.

'Oh, oh!' squealed the first little pig.

'Help, help!' squeaked the second little pig. But the third little pig was too busy stoking the fire.

'Ready or not, I'm coming!' laughed the Big Bad Wolf, and he slid down the chimney—straight into the bubbling, boiling pot . . .

Splash!

And that was the end of the Big Bad Wolf, thank goodness.

THE GINGERBREAD MAN

❖

A little old woman and a little old man both lived together in a little old house, and every now and then they were a little bit sad. They were sad because they had no children of their own. Now the little old woman wanted a child so much that one day she baked a little boy out of gingerbread.

He had orange peel for a mouth and raisins for eyes, and bright red cherries for his buttons. She tucked him up on rice paper, and put him in the oven to bake.

But when she lifted him out again—all plump and golden—he hopped off the baking tray and skipped out of the door. 'Husband! Husband! Come quick!' called the little old woman. 'Our son is running away!'

But though the little old woman ran after him, and the little old man ran after her, the gingerbread boy was too quick for them. As he ran, he looked over his shoulder and called:

'Run, run as fast as you can:
You can't catch me,
I'm the Gingerbread Man!'

He ran and ran, and as he ran the delicious smell of his golden suit reached a dog in a kennel. 'Stop! Stop, little Gingerbread Boy! I want to eat you up!' barked the dog, and chased after him.

But though the dog ran and ran, the gingerbread boy ran faster. He waved his hand and called out:

'I've run away from a little old woman and a little old man,
And I'll run away from you.
Run, run as fast as you can:
You can't catch me,
I'm the Gingerbread Man!'

He ran and ran, and as he ran the delicious smell of his golden suit reached a cow in a field. 'Stop! Stop, little Gingerbread Boy! I want to eat you up!' mooed the cow, and she trotted after him.

But though the cow ran and ran, the gingerbread boy ran faster. He thumbed his nose at the cow and called out:

'I've run away from a little old woman and a little old man, and a dog,
And I'll run away from you.
Run, run as fast as you can:
You can't catch me,
I'm the Gingerbread Man!'

He ran and ran, and as he ran the delicious smell of his golden suit reached a horse in a stable. 'Stop! Stop, little Gingerbread Boy! I want to eat you up!' neighed the horse, and galloped after him.

But though the horse ran and ran, the gingerbread boy ran faster. He laughed out loud and called:

'I've run away from a little old woman and a
little old man, a dog and a cow,
   And I'll run away from you.
   Run, run as fast as you can:
   You can't catch me,
   I'm the Gingerbread Man!'

He ran and ran, and as he ran the delicious smell of
his golden suit reached a little boy sitting on a gate.
'Stop! Stop, little Gingerbread Boy! I want to eat you up!'
shouted the little boy, and chased after him.

But though the little boy ran and ran, the gingerbread
boy ran faster. He stuck out his tongue and called:

'I've run away from a little old woman and a
little old man, a dog and a cow and a horse,
   And I'll run away from you.
   Run, run as fast as you can:
   You can't catch me,
   I'm the Gingerbread Man!'

He ran and ran, and as he ran the delicious smell of his golden suit reached the nose of a thin red fox, who leapt out of a ditch. The gingerbread boy hopped and skipped in front of him and laughed out loud:

'I've run away from a little old woman and a little old man, a dog and a cow,
a horse and a little boy, too,
And I'll run away from you.
Run, run as fast as you can:
You can't catch me,
I'm the Gingerbread Man!'

But the fox panted, 'You're quite mistaken, friend. I'm running away myself—from the huntsmen's hounds. I'll escape across the river, but what will you do?'

At that moment, they came to the bank of a wide, deep and rushing river. Behind them came the little boy and the horse and the cow and the dog and the little old man and his little old wife. For the first time in his little life, the gingerbread boy stopped bragging.

'Jump on to my tail,' said the fox, 'and I'll swim to the other side. What? Don't you trust me? How can I eat you if you're on my tail?' So the gingerbread boy jumped on to the fox's tail, and the fox plunged into the water.

How the gingerbread boy called and laughed and waved and thumbed his nose at the people and animals on the bank. 'I've run away from ALL of you!' he cried.

But a quarter of the way across the river, the fox said, 'Oh. Ow. You're heavy. Move up on to my back or I may drop you in the water.' So the gingerbread boy jumped on the fox's back.

But halfway across the river, the fox said, 'Oh. Ow. I'm getting very tired. Move up on to my shoulder or I may drop you in the water.' So the gingerbread boy jumped on to the fox's shoulder.

But three-quarters of the way across the river, the fox said, 'Oh. Ow. I'm sinking! Move up on to my head or I may drown you.'

So the gingerbread boy jumped on to the fox's head, and his feet were still quite dry when they reached the far bank. 'Now I'm safe!' he crowed. 'What a clever little Gingerbread Man I am!'

But as the fox climbed out of the river, he gave a flick of his head and tossed the gingerbread boy high in the air.

'Yap, snap!' went the fox.

'Oh dear!' cried the gingerbread boy. 'I'm quarter gone!'

'Gobble, gobble,' went the fox.

'Oh my!' cried the gingerbread boy. 'I'm half gone!'

'Yum, yum,' went the fox.

'Oh bother!' cried the gingerbread boy. 'I'm three-quarters gone!'

'Mmmm!' went the fox.

But the gingerbread boy said nothing at all.

'All gone,' said the fox, licking his lips.

THE BREMEN TOWN MUSICIANS

❖

A farmer once had a donkey, and the donkey worked on a farm. All life long he worked, until he was weary and weak at the knees. Then one morning, he heard his master say, 'That old donkey of mine is getting too old to work. I'll have to buy a younger one.'

'Oh dear, oh dear,' thought the donkey. 'Whatever will become of me? I must run away before the farmer sells me for dog meat.'

'But where will you go?' asked the other farm animals.

'I'll go to Bremen Town and play a violin in the streets and be a musician.'

He had not gone far when he tripped over a hound, sprawled in the roadway. 'What's your trouble?' he asked the hound. 'You look worn out.'

'That's what I am—worn out like an old doormat!' howled the dog pitifully. 'I'm getting so old that I can't

keep up with the other hounds when they're out hunting. Soon my master will sell me. I must get away. But what am I good for? What will become of me?'

'You look as if you could play the trombone if you put your mind to it,' said the donkey cheerfully. 'Come to Bremen Town with me. I'm going to start up a band.'

The hound gave a happy bark, and together they trotted on down the road.

But soon they met a cat, clinging to the branch of a tree and yowling miserably. 'What's your trouble?' asked the hound. 'You look frightened half to death.'

'Oiow! Oiow! I am! My mistress wants to drown me because I can't catch mice any more. I'm getting old, you see, and I'm slowing down. Besides, my eyesight isn't what it was. Oiow! Whatever will become of me?'

'You look as if you could play the drum as well as anyone,' said the hound. 'Come to Bremen Town with us. We're going to start up a band.'

The cat gave a happy miaow, and together the three trotted on down the road. Soon they passed a gate where a cock sat fluffed up like an old feather duster. 'What's your trouble?' asked the cat. 'You look a sorry sight.'

'I'm trying to keep awake,' said the cock. 'I daren't go to sleep or I may oversleep in the morning and not crow. Then the farmer will oversleep too, and blame me. He might wring my neck. Oh-bk! Oh-bk! It's a dreadful thing to grow old. Whatever will become of me?'

'Why not come to Bremen Town and sing for us?' said the cat. 'We're going to start up a band.'

The cock gave a happy *cock-a-doodle-dah*, and together the four trotted on down the road.

But Bremen Town proved to be much further away than they thought. By nightfall they were still in the heart of the countryside with not a town in sight.

'There's a light over there, beyond the trees,' said the donkey. 'Perhaps it's a farm with a barn where we can shelter for the night.'

The light came from a small house, and when the

animals got close to it, they could not
resist taking a peep through the window.
The cock stood on the cat's back. The cat
stood on the hound's back, and the hound
stood on the donkey's back. That way, the
cock could see over the window-sill.

Inside, by the light of a candle, three
robbers were eating a huge, delicious meal.
'Ooh-bk!' said the cock. 'There's food enough
for four and four more besides. You ought
to see!'

Then all four animals remembered
how hungry they were. The donkey said,
'We're on our way to Bremen to
become musicians. Why don't we
practise our music here, under this
window? Perhaps the kind men will like
our song and give us something to eat.'

Little did they know that this was the house of Murderous Max and his band of robbers—the wickedest robbers in the land!

Little did the robbers know what was in store for them when the Musicians of Bremen began to sing.

The donkey brayed, the cat yowled, the hound barked, and the cock crowed. All together, the sound was so terrible that the robbers thought the end of the world had come and leapt to their feet.

Then the hound toppled off the donkey. The cat toppled off the hound. The cock toppled off the cat and—*smash*—broke the window with the most enormous crash.

The robbers took to their heels and ran—out of the front door, out of the back door—and they did not stop running till they reached a wood and climbed three trees and stopped to listen. 'Have we escaped?'

'What was it?'

'Police?'

'Goblins?'

'Ghosts?'

They hid in the trees and waited. But no one had followed them into the wood. 'Perhaps it was nothing.'

'Perhaps it was only owls . . .'

'. . . or foxes in the dustbin.'

'We were fools to run away from a bit of noise.'

'One of us should go back and have a look.'

So Murderous Max climbed out of his tree and crept back to the house.

Meanwhile, the animals, finding themselves alone in the house, looked at the food and thought, 'Pity to waste it.' So they ate everything on the table. Feeling very weary after their long walk, they quickly fell asleep—the cat in the unlit grate, the hound by the door, the donkey in the yard, and the cock high in the rafters. The candles guttered and went out.

The whole house was sunk in darkness, when Murderous Max lifted the latch and crept inside. He saw a glitter in the hearth and thought it was the embers of a fire. 'I'll light a candle,' he thought—and poked the wick of a candle right in the cat's eye!

'Hsst-pssst!' said the cat, flew at the robber, and scratched his face.

The robber leapt back on to something he took for the doormat—until it got up and said 'Grrrow!' and bit him on the ankle.

Stricken with terror, the robber fled into the moonless yard—and collided with the donkey, waking him out of a deep sleep. It's hard to say who was more frightened, but the donkey kicked up his heels and caught the robber—*wham! blam!*—with his two hard hoofs.

Up in the rafters, the cock was woken by the robber's shriek, thought he was back on the farm, and crowed for all he was worth, '*COCK-A-DOODLE-DAH!*'

The robber scooted back to the wood, almost outrunning his own feet, and scuttled up his tree and would not speak for at least five minutes.

'Well?' said the others. 'Is there someone in the house? Is it safe to go back?'

'Never!' gasped Murderous Max. 'There's a witch up the chimney who scratched me with her nails. There's a thug behind the door who stabbed me with a carving knife. There's a huge black monster in the yard who thumped me with a club. And then a giant—as tall as the roof itself—shouted, "*STOP WHOEVER YOU ARE!*" I tell you, I'm never going back to that house as long as I live!'

So the robbers left that part of the world. The four animals stayed on in the house, waiting for the owners to come home. When, after a year, nobody had come, they put off their trip to Bremen Town and decided not to be musicians, after all. They simply sang to each other for fun in the evenings.

THE WOLF AND THE
SEVEN LITTLE KIDS

❖

Somewhere in the heart of a weary, wolfish world lived a mother goat and her seven little kids. And she loved those kids seven times more than she loved each one. So, when she set off for the market one day, she said, 'Lock the door behind me and don't open it to anyone's knocking. The Wicked Wolf would eat you if he could, and he'll try every trick to get in. He may pretend to be me, but you'll know him by his rough tough voice and his fat black paws.' Then she kissed each of the seven little kids and went on her way.

From the shadow of a nearby wood, the Wicked Wolf saw her go. 'So! Those seven little kids are all alone in the cottage! What a fine dinner for a hungry wolf!'

He knocked on the door of Goat Cottage: *rat–tat*. 'Who's there?'

The wolf put his paws on the door and growled, 'Children, children, open the door. It's your own little mother and I've brought seven presents, one for each of you. Open the door, why don't you?'

'No, no, we won't open the door,' cried the eldest kid. 'For you are not our little mother. Your voice is rough and tough and you are the Wicked Wolf!'

'Drat,' said the Wolf and went away.

He went to the shop and bought a stick of chalk and ate it. It made his voice not rough and tough, but soft and smooth, and back he went to Goat Cottage.

He knocked on the door: *rat-tat.*

'Who's there?'

The wolf put his paws on the window-sill and bleated, 'Children, children, open the door. It's your own little mother and I've brought seven presents, one for each of you. Open the door, do.'

'No, no, we won't open the door!' cried the eldest kid. 'For you are not our little mother. Your feet are fat and black, and you are the Wicked Wolf.'

'Drat,' said the Wolf and went away.

He went to the Miller and said, 'Put flour on my feet.'

'No, no, I won't put flour on your feet!' cried the Miller. 'You are up to your wicked tricks again.'

'Put flour on my feet, or I'll bite off your head,' said the Wolf. So the Miller put flour on the Wolf's feet, and back he went to Goat Cottage.

He knocked at the window: *rat-tat.*

'Who's there?'

Then the Wolf leaned his white paws on the window-sill and bleated, 'Children, children, open the door. It's your own little mother and I've brought seven presents, one for each of you. Open the door, do.'

'Yes, yes, and what's my present?' said the youngest

little kid . . . and opened the cottage door!

How those poor little kids scattered and scurried and hid.

One hid under the table.
One hid in the bed.
One hid in the wash-tub.
One in the kitchen, instead.
One hid in the oven, one
In the cupboard without a lock,
And one hid in the great big
Tall grandfather clock.

With a snarl and a sniff, the Wolf galloped about the cottage.

He found the kid under the table,

In the cupboard without a lock,

In the kitchen, the tub, the bed, and the stove

—But not the one in the clock.

Well, he wolfed down the six little kids and then, because he was full, he went out to sleep in the garden, under a tree.

No sooner had the back door shut than the front door opened, and in came the kids' own little mother. She saw the bed overturned and the cupboard opened wide, but no sign of her seven little kids. 'Owowo, what has become of my seven little kids?' and she called them one by one.

No answer came from the bed or tub,
From the cupboard without a lock,
From the table, the stove, or the kitchen,
—But an answer came from the clock.

'Owowo, little mother, I'm in the great big tall grandfather clock where I hid from the Wicked Wolf. But he ate up all my brothers and sisters—owowowo!'

At first the mother goat wept bitterly for her six little kids. Then she fetched the pepper pot from the kitchen and she went in search of the Wicked Wolf.

He was sleeping under the tree, his shaggy coat stretched out of shape by his dinner.

Creeping right up close and closer still, the mother goat tipped up the pepper pot and gave it six shakes over the Wolf's nose. Then she crept well away and further still, and put her hooves in her ears.

'AAtchoo! sneezed the Wolf.
'AatchOO!
AAtchOO!
AATCHOO!
AAATCHOOO!
AAATCHTCHOOO!'

And with every sneeze, out flew a little kid, bleating and blinking and *bump!*

'Oh, Maa! The Wolf was so greedy that he wolfed us down whole,' said the eldest. Then home ran the whole family, and bolted the door, and danced with joy because they were all together again.

'AAAATCHOOOO!' said the Wolf, and he sneezed himself tail-over-ears out of the garden and halfway home.

Between sneezes he thought, 'That's the last time I eat kids for supper! It's plain—AH—it's plain they don't agree with—A-A-A-A-T-H-C-T-C-H-O-O-O-!!!—me.'

THE OLD WOMAN AND HER PIG

❖

One day an old woman was sweeping her yard when she found a crooked sixpence.

'Aha!' cried her cat. 'Now you can afford to pour me a saucer of milk!'

'Oh, no!' said the old woman. 'Now I can go to market and buy a fat pig!' And that's what she did. But on her way home with the sixpenny pig, she came to a stile in a fence.

'Pig, pig, climb over the stile,
Or I shan't get home tonight.'
But the pig would not.

So the old woman left her sixpenny pig by the stile and went on down the road to look for help. She found a dog sleeping in the sun.

She said to the dog:
'Dog, dog, bite pig—
Pig won't climb over the stile
And I shan't get home tonight.'
But the dog would not.

So the old woman picked up a stick that lay nearby.

'Stick, stick, strike dog—

Dog won't bite pig,

Pig won't climb over the stile

And I shan't get home tonight.'

But the stick would not.

So the old woman went a little further down the road to look for help. Soon she came to a fire.

She said to the fire:

'Fire, fire, burn stick—

Stick won't strike dog,

Dog won't bite pig,

Pig won't climb over the stile

And I shan't get home tonight.'

But the fire would not.

So the old woman went a little further down the road to look for help. Soon she came to a bucket of water.

She said to the bucket of water:

'Water, water, put out fire—

Fire won't burn stick,

Stick won't strike dog,

Dog won't bite pig,

Pig won't climb over the stile

51

And I shan't get home tonight.'
But the bucket of water would not.

So the old woman went a little further down the road to look for help. Soon she met a cow.

She said to the cow:
'Cow, cow, drink water—
Water won't put out fire,
Fire won't burn stick,
Stick won't strike dog,
Dog won't bite pig,
Pig won't climb over the stile
And I shan't get home tonight.'
But the cow would not.

So the old woman went a little further down the road to look for help. Soon she met a butcher.

She said to the butcher:
'Butcher, butcher, drive cow—
Cow won't drink water,
Water won't put out fire,
Fire won't burn stick,
Stick won't strike dog,
Dog won't bite pig,
Pig won't climb over the stile
And I shan't get home tonight.'

But the butcher would not.

So the old woman went a little further down the road to look for help. Soon she met a rope coiled up like a snake.

She said to the rope:
'Rope, rope, bind butcher—
Butcher won't drive cow,
Cow won't drink water,
Water won't put out fire,
Fire won't burn stick,
Stick won't strike dog,
Dog won't bite pig,
Pig won't climb over the stile
And I shan't get home tonight.'
But the rope would not.

So the old woman went a little further down the road to look for help. Soon she met a black rat.

She said to the black rat:
'Rat, rat, gnaw rope—
Rope won't bind butcher,
Butcher won't drive cow,
Cow won't drink water,
Water won't put out fire,
Fire won't burn stick,

Stick won't strike dog,
Dog won't bite pig,
Pig won't climb over the stile
And I shan't get home tonight.'
But the rat would not.

So the old woman went a little further down the road to look for help. In fact she got all the way home, and found her cat sleeping on the fence.

She said to the cat:
'Cat, cat, chase rat—
Rat won't gnaw rope,
Rope won't bind butcher,
Butcher won't drive cow,
Cow won't drink water,
Water won't put out fire,
Fire won't burn stick,
Stick won't strike dog,
Dog won't bite pig,

Pig won't climb over the stile
And I shan't get home tonight.'
The cat look at her with one green
eye and then with the other. 'Give me a
saucer of milk and I will chase the
rat,' she said.

So the old woman fetched a
saucer of milk and gave it to
the cat who drank it.

Then the cat licked her whiskers,
walked down the road, and began to
chase the rat. The rat began to gnaw
the rope. The rope began to bind the
butcher. The butcher began to drive
the cow. The cow began to drink the

water. The water began to put out the fire. The
fire began to burn the stick. The stick began
to strike the dog. The dog began to bite
the pig—and with one bound the
pig jumped right over the stile!

So the old woman *did* get home
that night.

And the cat did get her milk.

GOLDILOCKS AND THE THREE BEARS

❖

One morning three bears sat down to breakfast. There was a great big Daddy Bear, middling big Mummy Bear, and Baby Bear, who was no bigger than you. Mummy Bear served their porridge into three bowls—one great big bowl, one middling big bowl, and one no bigger than a teacup. But it was too hot to eat right away.

'Let's go for a walk while it cools,' said Daddy Bear. So that's what they did.

No sooner had they set off into the wood, than a little girl came walking through the trees. When she tossed her head, golden ringlets sprang round her shoulders. 'Oh dear, oh dear,' said Goldilocks. 'Wherever can I be? I only stepped into the wood to pick some flowers, and now I'm as lost as lost. I know—I'll ask at this house if they know the way home.'

But as she knocked at the cottage door, it swung open under her fist, and there was the kitchen, all warm and cosy. A delicious smell of cooking greeted her. 'I'm so hungry!' thought Goldilocks.

On the kitchen table were three bowls of porridge— one great big bowl, one middling big bowl, and one no bigger than a teacup. So, without asking or being asked, Goldilocks took a taste from the great big bowl.

'Ouch! That's much too hot!' So she took a taste from the middling big bowl, but 'Ugh! That's much too salty!' So she took a taste from the littlest bowl, and that was just right. In fact it was so good that she ate it all up, without asking or being asked.

'Phew! I'm tired,' thought Goldilocks. 'I'll just sit down for a while. Perhaps the people who live here will come home.'

Pulled up to the table were three chairs—one great big chair, one middling big chair, and one no bigger than her own little chair at home. So without asking or being asked, Goldilocks sat down in the great big chair.

'Oh no, this is much too high.' So she sat down in the middling big chair, but, 'Oh dear, this is much too hard.' So she sat down in the littlest chair—and that was just right. In fact it was so like her own little chair at home that she drummed and drummed her heels until— CRASH—the chair fell all to pieces!

When Goldilocks picked herself up, she felt very cross and weary. 'I'm too tired to try and mend it. I think I'll just go and have a sleep.'

Goldilocks climbed the stairs, and found a bedroom with three beds in it. There was one great big bed, and one middling big bed, and one no bigger than her own little bed at home. So, without asking or being asked, she climbed up on to the great big bed.

'Oh dear, this is much too lumpy!' So she climbed on to the middling big bed, but, 'Oh dear, this is much too soft.' So she climbed on to the littlest bed—and that was just right. In fact it was so comfortable that she dozed off. So she did not hear the pad-pad of paws on the path, the turn of the doorhandle, the creak of the kitchen door as the three bears came home from their walk!

The moment he stepped into the kitchen, Daddy Bear held up a great big paw. 'What's this? What's this? Someone's been eating my porridge!' he roared in his deep, dark voice.

'And someone's been eating my porridge,' said Mummy Bear in her golden-brown voice.

'Someone's been eating my porridge!' squeaked Baby Bear. 'And they've eaten it all up!'

'Never mind,' said Mummy Bear. 'Sit down and you can share Daddy's.'

But when they went to sit down, Daddy Bear held up a great big paw. 'What's this? What's this? Someone's been sitting in my chair!' he roared in his deep, dark voice.

'And someone's been sitting in my chair,' said Mummy Bear in her golden-brown voice.

'Someone's been sitting in my chair,' squealed Baby Bear. 'And they've broken it all to pieces!'

'There, there,' said Mummy Bear.

'Hrmph!' said Daddy Bear. Step by step and stair by stair, he crept upstairs on his great big paws. Mummy Bear crept after him, and Baby Bear came up behind.

Silently, with one great paw, Daddy Bear opened the bedroom door and looked inside.

'What's this? What's this? Someone's been sleeping in my bed!' he roared in his deep, dark voice.

'And someone's been sleeping in my bed!' said Mummy Bear in her golden-brown voice.

'Someone's been sleeping in my bed!' whimpered Baby Bear. 'And she's still there!'

At that very moment, Goldilocks opened her eyes, and saw in front of her three bears—one great big bear, one middling big bear, and one no bigger than herself. But they were all *very* angry.

She gave a piercing scream and jumped clean out of the window on to a pile of leaves below. Without asking or being asked, she ran and ran and did not stop running till she found her way home.

'Well, well!' roared Daddy Bear in his deep, dark voice.

'There, there,' said Mummy Bear in her golden-brown voice.

'I'm hungry,' said Baby Bear. 'Let's have breakfast.'

THE LITTLE RED HEN

❖

Once upon a time a little red hen lived in a farmyard. One day she found some grains of wheat and showed them to the other animals—a duck, a cat, and a dog. 'Who will help me plant these grains of wheat?' she asked.

'Not I,' said the Duck.

'Not I,' said the Cat.

'Not I,' said the Dog.

'Very well,' said the Little Red Hen. 'I'll plant them myself.'

So she did.

The sun shone and the rain fell, and slowly, slowly, little green shoots sprang from the dark soil. When the wheat was tall and golden, the Little Red Hen said, 'Who will help me cut the wheat?'

'Not today,' said the Duck.

'Not today,' said the Cat.

'Not today,' said the Dog.

'Very well,' said the Little Red Hen. 'I'll cut it myself.'

So she did.

The cut wheat lay on the barn floor, heavy with husks. 'Who will help me thresh the wheat?' asked the Little Red Hen.

'No thanks,' said the Duck.

'No thanks,' said the Cat.

'No thanks,' said the Dog.

'Very well,' said the Little Red Hen. 'I'll thresh it myself.'

So she did.

'The wheat is ready for grinding,' said the Little Red Hen. 'Who will take it to the mill?'

'Too far,' said the Duck.

'Too far,' said the Cat.

'Too far,' said the Dog.

'Very well,' said the Little Red Hen. 'I'll take it myself.'

So she did.

The Little Red Hen took the wheat up the hill to the mill, where the miller ground it into flour. 'Here's the flour,' said the Little Red Hen when she got home. 'Who will help me bake it into bread?'

'Not I,' said the Duck.

'Not I,' said the Cat.

'Not I,' said the Dog.

'Very well,' said the Little Red Hen. 'I'll bake it myself.'

So she did.

She kneaded the flour into dough, then put it into a hot oven until it was golden brown.

'The bread's baked,' said the Little Red Hen. 'Who will help me eat it?'

'I will,' said the Duck.

'I will,' said the Cat.

'I will,' said the Dog.

'Oh no you won't!' said the Little Red Hen. 'I'll do that myself.'

So she did.

THE MAGIC PORRIDGE POT

❖

There was once a time so hard that everyone went hungry. In one particular village, in one particular house, there was no food at all.

A little girl called Kasha lived there with her mother. Every day, Kasha collected berries in the wood and mushrooms in the field, and enough herbs for a pot of tea.

But as the summer turned to autumn, and the autumn leaves fell, the hungry birds ate the last of the berries, and no more mushrooms grew. One day, Kasha took her mother's basket into the woods, but found no food at all. She stood beneath a tree as it wept its dead leaves to the ground, and her own tears dropped on to the fallen leaves.

Rap-tap—a gnarled stick of wood tapped her on the shoulder. *Jab*—the walking stick poked her in the back. 'What are you crying for?' croaked a crotchety old voice. 'Think you've got troubles? Don't you know, there's always someone worse off than you?'

Kasha quickly dried her eyes. 'Yes, yes. Of course.'

'Look at me, for instance. I've got to carry this heavy cooking pot, and I'm far too old to be carrying heavy cast-iron cooking pots around the world.'

'Let me carry it for you a little way,' said Kasha smiling. The old lady's cooking pot certainly was heavy; it was all Kasha could do to carry it.

'That's better!' said the old woman, without a word of thanks. 'I know, you look after it for me. I have to go on a trip. I'll come back for it later. Use it, if you like. Or don't. I don't care.'

'I just wish we had anything to cook in it,' Kasha thought aloud as she struggled along, trying to keep up with the old lady.

'Don't you go putting mucky *food* in it, my girl. "Cook, pot, cook"—that's all you have to say. And "Stop, pot, stop" when it's done. Even you can remember that, can't you?'

'Slow down, please. I can't keep up!' called Kasha. But the old lady hurried on ahead without a backward glance, and was soon lost from sight among the trees. Kasha turned home towards the village, the iron pot banging and thumping against her hip. 'I wonder . . .' she thought. 'I wonder . . .'

'Help me put this on the table, Mother,' said Kasha when she got home. 'Then fetch two bowls.'

'Bless us, child, where did you get that dirty old thing? Where are the berries for supper? What, no mushrooms? What have you been up to, you naughty, lazy girl?'

So Kasha lifted the pot on to the table herself, and said to it, 'Cook, pot, cook!'

There was a hollow ringing, then a wet trickling, then a steamy simmering, then a delicious bubbling—and the mouthwatering smell of PORRIDGE! Golden as wheat and laced with dark-brown honey—it foamed and fountained in the pot till there was enough for two, and more besides. Kasha's mother hurried away to fetch bowls. So she did not hear Kasha say to the little cooking pot, 'Stop, pot, stop!'

When she returned the bubbling had stopped.
'Wonderful! Wonderful!' cried the
mother over and over again, as she ladled
out the porridge and gulped it down with a
huge cooking spoon.

'Shall I invite the neighbours round for a
porridge party?' asked Kasha.

But her mother snapped, 'No!' and threw a towel over
the iron pot to hide it. 'No, this is ours. Who knows
when the magic might run out.'

Next day, they ate breakfast from the porridge pot,
and lunch too. Then Kasha went out to play. Her friends
lived at the very top of the town. 'Now don't you go
telling your friends about my magic porridge pot, will
you?' her mother called after her.

When Kasha was out of sight, her mother sat down
in the kitchen and stared at the wonderful pot hidden
under its towel. She took off the towel and stared even
longer. She polished the pot and oiled its iron handle.
The very sight of it made her hungry.

'Now what was it Kasha said? "Cook, pot, cook!"
That was it. Cook, pot . . . oh!' The magic words had
already been spoken and already the pot was half-full of
porridge. 'Wonderful! Magnificent!' cried the mother,
eating straight from the pot. 'Right, that's enough, thank
you.'

The pot took no notice. It went right on bubbling.

'No more now, thank you,' she said.

But the pot went on making porridge.

'That's enough, I said!'

But the porridge brimmed over on to the table.

'Oh, my clean tablecloth!' squealed Kasha's mother. 'Don't, pot, don't!'

The fountain of porridge welled over the table edge and began to spread across the kitchen floor.

'Oh, pot, oh!' wailed Kasha's mother, ankle-deep in porridge. But the pot took no notice. It went on and on

and on boiling up the delicious golden mixture laced with brownest honey.

'Yuck, pot, ugh!' said the mother, wading knee-deep. The table was soon afloat, and the porridge pot sailed up through the house on a tide of porridge.

'No, pot, no!' shrieked the mother, running upstairs to escape the flood. 'Please, pot, please!'

Soon there was porridge bubbling up the chimney and spilling out of the windows. Passers-by in the street were washed off their feet by the surging porridge. They clung to letter boxes, trees, and rooftops, as the village disappeared under a sea of porridge.

At the top of the town, Kasha heard the commotion and ran out of doors. She was in time to see the porridge breaking in waves over the Town Hall roof.

She guessed at once what had happened. So, climbing into a wash-tub, she paddled down the town. In the far distance, she could hear her mother shouting, 'Halt, pot, halt! Glug, pot, glug-glug-glug!'

'Stop, pot, stop!' called Kasha, and fortunately the pot heard her. The waves stilled; the bubbling stopped; the porridge lay shimmering under the setting sun.

The hungry villagers began at the top of the town and ate their way through every mouthful. It took them all winter, and they never once complained, because the

magic porridge was so delicious.

In the spring, Kasha was picking berries and mushrooms on the edge of the wood. (They made a pleasant change from porridge.) She sang and danced as she went.

Rap-tap—a gnarled stick of wood tapped her on the shoulder. *Jab*—the walking stick poked her in the back. 'What are you looking so happy about?' croaked a crotchety old voice. 'There are plenty of people in the world happier than you.'

Kasha grinned more broadly. 'I'm very glad to hear it. Now come back to my house, and I'll give you your magic cooking pot and a cup of tea.' And throwing her arms round the old witch, Kasha kissed her. 'Thank you! You gave us food for the whole winter!'

'Just my little joke,' croaked the witch. Then she burst into such a fit of giggles that she had to sit down on a tree stump. 'Do you know what I saw as I came past the village? Dried porridge round the church spire!'

Then Kasha began to giggle, too, and they both sat on the tree stump and laughed until their salt tears fell on the spring grass. Later, the old witch collected her cooking pot from Kasha's kitchen, and flew away with it on Kasha's mother's best broomstick.

THE GOLDEN GOOSE

❖

Once when the forester needed firewood, he said to his first and second sons, 'Go into the forest and cut down a tree.'

'Can I go, too?' said the third son, called Simpleton.

'You're too silly,' said the forester.

'You're too clumsy,' said the first son.

'You're too stupid,' said the second son.

But Simpleton went anyway.

Each boy took lunch and a drink, but they had only one axe between them, so they took it in turns to chop. The eldest boy began.

At the first stroke of the axe, a little grey man stepped out from behind the tree. 'Give me a bite to eat and a drop to drink,' he said.

'Certainly not. I haven't got any food or drink with me. Go on, push off! Ow! Now look what you made me do!' He had dropped the axe on his foot, and he limped home howling.

So the second son picked up the axe. 'Give me a bite to eat and a drop to drink,' said the little grey man to the second son.

'Certainly not. I haven't got anything to spare. Go on, push off! Ow! Now look what you made me do!' He had hit himself over the head with the axe, and he went home wailing.

So the third brother—the one called Simpleton— picked up the axe and started chopping. 'Give me a bite to eat and a drop to drink,' said the little grey man.

'Of course,' said Simpleton. 'There's nothing but cheese rind and stale crust and water, but you're welcome to share it with me.'

They sat down on a log and ate and drank. And funnily enough, the rind tasted like soft, fat cheese, and the bread tasted crumbly and fresh-baked, and the water tasted like cider.

'If I were you,' said the grey old man as he munched, 'I'd chop down that tree over there.'

So that's what Simpleton did.

As the tree fell, a shiny yellow bird ran out from among the roots, and Simpleton caught it up in his arms. 'A golden goose!' he cried. 'I'll go and show the King!'

So Simpleton set off, with the golden goose tucked under his arm, and stopped for the night at an inn.

Now the innkeeper had three daughters, and the eldest brought Simpleton his supper. She saw the golden goose under Simpleton's arm and she said to herself, 'That bird could spare one feather to make me rich.'

So when Simpleton got up to go to bed, she crept up behind him to snatch a golden feather. But from the moment she laid hands on the golden goose, she could not let go!

Up the stairs went Simpleton, and never once looked round, so he did not know that the innkeeper's daughter was following on behind. Her younger sister said to herself, 'If Floribunda is after a feather, I'll take one, too!' And she caught hold of her sister to pull her aside.

But from the moment she laid hands on her sister, she could not let go!

The youngest sister said to herself, 'If Eglantine is after a feather, I'll take one, too.' And she caught hold of her sister to pull her aside. But from the moment she laid hands on Eglantine, she could not let go! So Simpleton went to bed, with the goose tucked under his arm, and the three girls had to follow on behind. It was a very uncomfortable night.

Next morning, Simpleton set off, and never once looked round, so he did not see the three girls following on behind. The vicar saw them stumbling across a field and called out, 'Floribunda! Eglantine! Aspidistra! Come away! Fancy chasing after that young man! What would your mother say?' And he tried to pull them away.

But from the moment he laid hands on Aspidistra, he could not let go, and like it or not, he had to follow on behind.

As they passed the church, the sexton called out, 'Vicar! What are you doing holding that girl's hand? And you a man of the cloth! What would your wife say? Besides, you've got a christening at two. The babies are already in the church!' And running after the vicar, he tried to pull him away.

But from the moment he laid hands on the vicar, he

could not let go, and like it or not, he had to follow on behind.

As they passed a farm, the sexton called out to a couple of farm-hands, 'Help me! I'm stuck!' The farm-hands ran out and tried to pull the sexton away. But from the moment they laid hands on the sexton, they could not let go, and like it or not, they had to follow on behind.

So Simpleton went on his way, and never once looked round, so he did not see the seven who trotted along behind. He came at last to the King's palace. And who should be looking out of the window but the Sad Princess.

Now the Sad Princess was the King's only daughter. All her life she had been so sad that the King vowed, 'If anyone can make her smile, he shall marry her—and have half my kingdom, too!'

Below the window of the Sad Princess trotted Simpleton, clutching the golden goose under his arm. And behind Simpleton trotted the innkeeper's three daughters, the vicar, the sexton, and the two farm-hands, all glued as close together as the letters in a word.

'Oh, Father! Father! Come and see!' called the Sad Princess. 'Isn't this the funniest sight you ever saw?' And she laughed so much that she almost toppled out of the window.

'Who has made my daughter laugh like this?' demanded the King. 'Let him come and claim his reward!'

But when the King saw Simpleton (and the innkeeper's three daughters and the vicar and the sexton and the two farm-hands) he did not want to keep his promise. 'They call you Simpleton,' he said. 'Unless you are clever enough to drink all the wine in my cellar, I can't give you my daughter or half my kingdom!'

Simpleton did not know what to do. 'I'll go and ask the little grey man in the forest,' he thought. 'He knew

where to find a golden goose, he may know how to drink all the King's wine.'

Back he went to the forest (and, of course, the innkeeper's three daughters and the vicar and the sexton and the two farm-hands followed on behind). He found the little grey man sitting on a log, crying. 'Oh dear, oh dear. I've drunk a river and I've drunk a pond, and still I'm thirsty!'

Simpleton told the little grey man about the King's wine, and off the man went at a run to drink up every last drop.

But by the time Simpleton got back (with the innkeeper's three daughters and the vicar and the sexton and the two farm-hands following on behind) the King did not want to keep his promise. 'They call you Simpleton,' he said. 'Unless this mountain of bread is eaten by morning, I can't give you my daughter or half my kingdom!'

Simpleton didn't know what to do. 'I'll go and ask the little grey man in the forest,' he thought. 'He knew where to find a golden goose and how to drink all the King's wine. He may know how to eat a mountain of bread.'

Back he went to the forest (and, of course, the innkeeper's three daughters and the vicar and the sexton and the two farm-hands followed on behind). He found the little grey man perched on a branch, sobbing. 'Oh dear, oh dear, I've eaten all the acorns and I've eaten all the nuts, and still I'm hungry!'

Simpleton told the little grey man about the mountain of bread and off the man went at a run to eat up every last crust and crumb.

But by the time Simpleton got back (with the innkeeper's three daughters and the vicar and the sexton and the two farm-hands following on behind) the King did not want to keep his promise. 'They call you Simpleton,' he said. 'Unless you come to your wedding in a boat that can sail on land or sea, I can't give you my daughter or half my kingdom!'

Simpleton did not know what to do. 'I'll go and ask

the little grey man in the forest,' he thought. 'He knew where to find a golden goose and how to drink all the King's wine and eat a mountain of bread. He may know how to build a boat that will sail on land and sea.'

Back he went to the forest (and, of course, the innkeeper's three daughters, and the vicar and the sexton and the two farm-hands followed on behind). He found the little grey man singing a song.

'Bread when I was hungry

Wine when I was dry

And yesterday a rind and crust:

I want to, will and can and must

Help you, friend, or try my best.'

Simpleton mentioned the boat that could sail on land and sea. The little grey man turned one somersault, and there stood a boat with oars inside and wheels on its keel, and in it they all sailed back to the King's palace.

When the King saw the boat coming, and in it Simpleton and the little grey man and the innkeeper's daughters and the vicar and the sexton and the two farm-hands, he knew he was beaten, and announced a royal wedding.

So Simpleton and the Princess were married. And though they had not meant to be there, Floribunda and Eglantine and Aspidistra and the vicar and the sexton and the two farm-hands were happy to sit in the front pews, minding the golden goose.

THE ELVES AND THE SHOEMAKER

❖

Work, work, work. In the little cobbler's shop at the end of the street, Alfred the shoemaker work-work-worked from daybreak till dusk. He stitched boots and shoes all day long, until the light grew too bad for him to see. But however hard he worked, he could not make enough money to live on.

'My old fingers are getting stiff,' he told his wife. 'I can't work as fast as I did.'

'Sew bigger stitches,' said his wife, 'then the shoes won't take so long to finish.'

'Oh dear me, no,' said Alfred. 'People come to me because they know my work is good. I won't make shoddy shoes.'

But soon the shoemaker had so little money that he could not afford to buy new leather.

'You can't make shoes without leather,' said his wife, 'and there's only enough left for one more pair of shoes. What then?'

'Something will turn up,' said Alfred, but he had to wipe the tears off his spectacles before he could go on sewing. That night, he lay awake, worrying.

In the morning, he set out his tools and sharpened his knife. Then he turned to his workbench to cut his last pair of shoes from the last piece of leather.

But there on the bench, instead, stood a finished pair of dancing shoes—as pretty a pair as ever danced a polka. 'Where did they come from, wife? Who made them? Look, here are the scraps of leather! Someone has cut and stitched my last pair of shoes!'

'And look at the size of the stitches!' said his wife. 'They're as small as grains of sugar! Put the shoes in the window at once—so that our customers can see them!'

The shoes had not been in the window half an hour, when the Duke himself came in and bought them for his daughter. He said the workmanship was so fine that he would recommend the cobbler to all his friends at Court.

'Quick! Drop everything!' cried the wife, when the Duke had gone. 'Take the money and buy leather—or the Duke's friends may come looking for shoes and we shall have none to sell!'

By evening, Alfred had bought leather enough for two pairs of shoes, but he barely had time to cut them out before nightfall.

In the morning, he came downstairs feeling much happier—and what do you think he found on his workbench? Not one pair of shoes, but two. Two pairs of button boots, as shiny as water, and sewn with stitches as small as grains of pepper.

Two fashionable ladies soon bought them, and promised to tell their friends about the shoemaker's shop.

'Quick! Drop everything!' cried Alfred's wife, when the ladies had gone. 'Take the money and buy leather!'

With the money from the button boots, Alfred bought leather enough for at least four pairs of shoes, but he did not have time to cut them out before nightfall.

Next morning, he came downstairs whistling for joy—and what do you think he found on his workbench? Not two pairs of shoes, but four, yes, four pairs of riding boots, as glossy as wax and sewn with stitches as small as grains of salt.

Four huntsmen bought the boots, and promised to tell all their friends about the shoemaker's shop.

Every day, Alfred could afford to buy more leather. Every night, his mysterious visitors made shoes from it. But never once did the shoemaker glimpse a stranger in his shop, working at his bench.

The Duke and the fashionable ladies and the huntsmen all told their friends about Alfred's shop, and soon there were customers coming and going all day long. The cobbler was richer than he had ever been before.

'This isn't fair, wife,' he said, one frosty day soon before Christmas. 'I'm growing rich, but somebody else is doing the work. And I don't even know who it is.'

So that night, they hid behind the shop counter and waited to see who came. At the stroke of midnight, when the snow was flying against the window, and the water in the vases was frozen solid, a little elf man poked his bare head out of a mousehole. He sped across the draughty floor, followed by five other elves, all hugging themselves against the cold.

They climbed on to the workbench up the string of Alfred's apron, and set to work, cutting and stretching and stitching and nailing and lacing and polishing a dozen pairs of shoes.

'The poor little mites!' whispered Alfred's wife. 'They've not a stitch to wear!'

It was true. The elves were blue with cold, and stamped their feet and clapped their hands as they worked, to keep them from going numb. As the first ray of sunshine crept through the frost on the windows, the elves ran back to their mousehole and disappeared from sight.

'I think I know how to repay their kindness,' said Alfred.

But his wife was already sorting through her sewing box. 'Here's cloth for trousers and felt for hats and boots. One of your handkerchiefs will make six shirts, I think . . .'

All day long she sewed, while Alfred cooked some steaming soup. That night he put away his leather and his tools, and left the elves' presents instead on the workbench, alongside a bowl of hot soup and a warm oil-lamp.

Once more, Alfred and his wife hid behind the counter.

As the church clock welcomed in Christmas Day, the six elves, without a stitch of clothing, darted across the shop floor and climbed on to the bench to begin work. They looked around, puzzled, when they found no leather to cut. Then their little faces broke into smiles as they realized that the presents were for them!

'A hat!' cried one.

'A shirt!' cried another.

'And velvet trousers, too!'

'We're smart fellows now!' crowed a little elf, admiring himself in the shiny oil-lamp.

'Too smart to work nights!' declared his friend.

'Let's go and see the world!'

And with that they danced out of the shop and into the Christmas snow, never to be seen again.

Alfred did not mind when the elves deserted his little shop. He had shoes enough for a hundred customers and leather enough for a lifetime. And on cold nights, he was glad that somewhere, out in the world, the kind little elves were warmer than before. But he kept one pair of elf shoes for himself, and never sold them—because he so admired those tiny stitches, small as grains of dust.